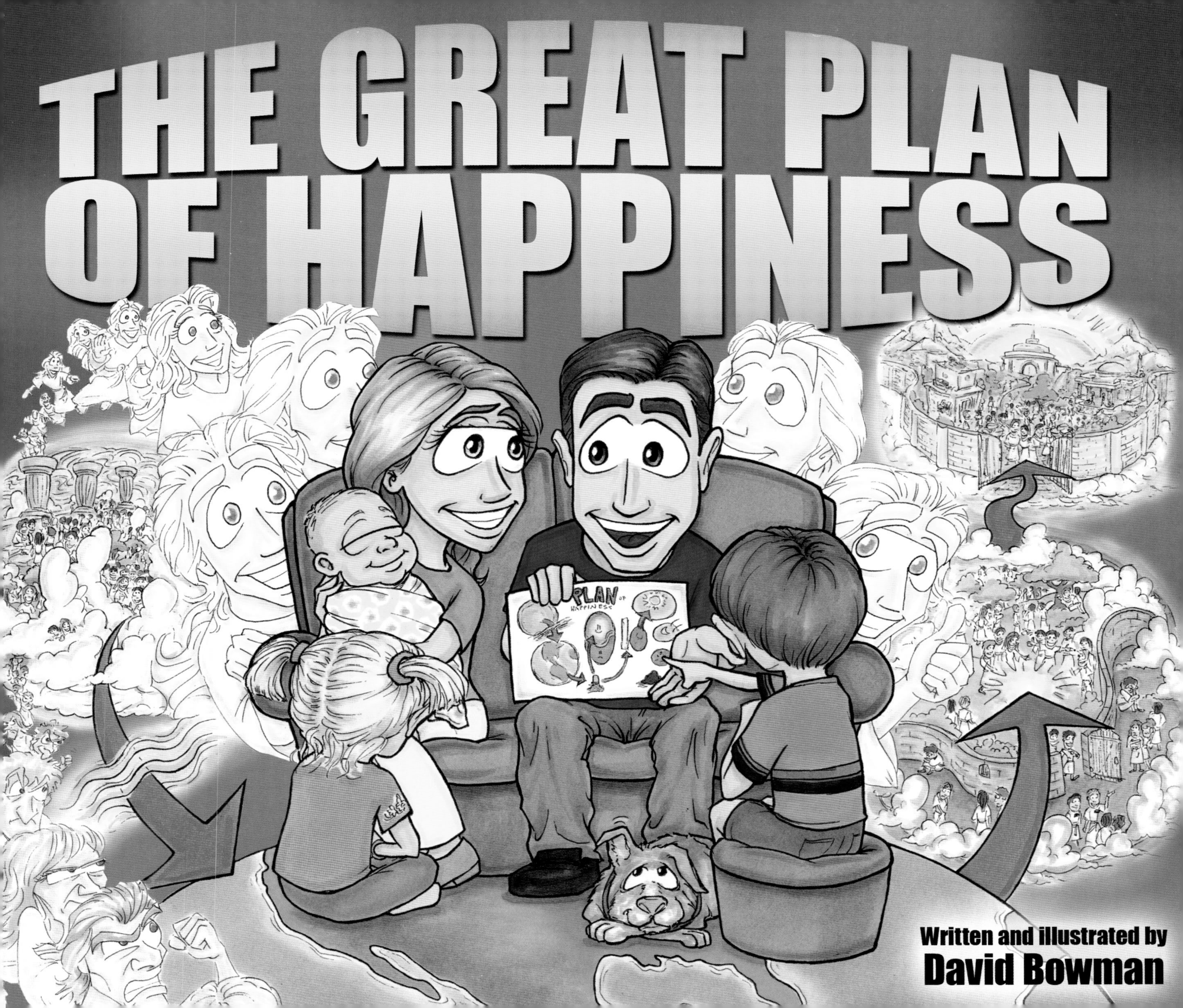
THE GREAT PLAN
OF HAPPINESS
Written and illustrated by
David Bowman

ISBN 13: 978-1-59955-451-8

Published by CFI, an imprint of Cedar Fort, Inc.
2373 W. 700 S., Springville, UT 84663
Distributed by Cedar Fort, Inc., www.cedarfort.com

LIBRARY OF CONGRESS CATALOGING-IN-PUBLICATION DATA

Bowman, David, 1974-
The great plan of happiness / David Bowman.
p. cm.
ISBN 978-1-59955-451-8
1. Salvation--Mormon Church--Juvenile literature. 2. Mormon Church--Doctrines--Juvenile literature. 3. Church of Jesus Christ of Latter-day Saints--Doctrines--Juvenile literature. I. Title.

BX8643.S25B69 2010
234--dc22

2010018943

Cover and book design by Tanya Quinlan
Edited by Melissa J. Caldwell
Cover design © 2010 by Lyle Mortimer

Printed on acid-free paper
Printed in China

10 9 8 7 6 5 4 3 2 1

## AUTHOR'S NOTE TO PARENTS

I love teaching about the Great Plan of Happiness. I hope this book helps you in teaching your children of their glorious roots and their glorious destiny. Obviously, I have had to take artistic license in my depictions of our premortal experience and the postmortal worlds, since we know so little of what these places and events actually look(ed) like. I have also taken artistic license in my depictions of Heavenly Father and have chosen to portray Him according to the artistic style of the book. However, I hope that these depictions are not perceived as lacking in reverence and respect for the sacred nature of Deity. Nothing could be further from the truth. My intent is simply to teach children, in the language of children (which is visual), about the reality of their loving Father in Heaven and His plan for them.

Do you ever wonder . . .

Where you were *before* you were born?

Where you will go *after* you die?

And
what you should be
doing here on earth?

These are very
important
questions.

YES, you DID live before you were born!

YES, you WILL keep living after you die!

So let's learn together about this exciting journey you are on. It began...

… a long, long, loooooong time ago, in the PREMORTAL WORLD.
You were a spirit son or daughter,
born of heavenly parents.
They loved you so much.
You were taught many important
things there.
SPIRIT

As you grew,
you gained special
talents and abilities
that made you
unique.
Hhhhmmm...
Hhhhmm...
However, you did not yet
have a body or
a fulness of joy
as your Heavenly Father
does.
You knew that one day
you *could* grow up
to be like your
heavenly parents,
but you would
need help.

So, one day, Heavenly Father gathered together all of His spirit children for a HUGE family home evening. You were there! At that gathering, He presented a plan that would help us to become as He is. It is sometimes called the Great Plan of Happiness or the Plan of Salvation.

He explained that each of us would go to a place called earth

and receive a physical body.

While on earth,
we would grow and learn
and have many new
experiences.

Heavenly Father
knew we would also
make mistakes . . .

so He chose His
eldest son, Jesus Christ,
to go to earth also and
become our Savior.

Because of our
oldest brother, Jesus,
it would be possible
for us to return to
our heavenly
parents.

We were so excited!
We all shouted for joy because of this Great Plan of Happiness!

You had another brother, named Lucifer.
Lucifer was selfish and wanted to change Heavenly Father's plan.
He persuaded many of your spirit brothers and sisters to follow him
These spirits rebelled against Fathe
For a long time, we encouraged them to support Father's plan.
TITLE OF AGENCY
GENERAL MICHAEL
We call this the "War in Heaven."

Finally, Lucifer and his followers were cast out. He became known as Satan, or the devil.
However, *you* were strong and faithful in choosing to follow Heavenly Father's Great Plan of Happiness.
You showed Father that you could be trusted.
He has never forgotten that.
THOSE WHO HAVE PROVEN THEY CAN BE TRUSTED

So why can't you remember any of this?
Because just as you came to earth, Heavenly Father put a **VEIL of forgetfulnes** over your memory of the premortal world.
Heavenly Father wanted your life on earth to be a test, to see if you would follow Him in faith . . .
even if you couldn't see Him or remember Him.
You went *through* this veil an then you were . . .

# Born!!

Happy Birthday to You!
Welcome to **EARTH!**

Your *spirit* went into a
tiny baby **body**.

You were born to earthly parents who would love, teach, and take care of you.
Your earthly family is one of your greatest helps
from your loving Father in Heaven.

And there are many more helps your Heavenly Father has given you for your life on earth: Your greatest help is your Savior, Jesus Christ.

He came to earth before you did. He gave us a perfect example to follow. Jesus paid for our sins, died, and was resurrected. This is called the Atonement. Because of Him, we will ALL be resurrected someday. Because of His great love, we can ALL repent of our sins and be worthy to return to Heavenly Father and become like Him.

Some other heavenly helps are:

PRAYER

Even though your Heavenly Father isn't here with you, He knows you and wants you to talk with Him. That's how He can stay close to you and bless you while you are away from Him.

THE CHURCH

Jesus Christ's Church helps us in many ways because it gives us:

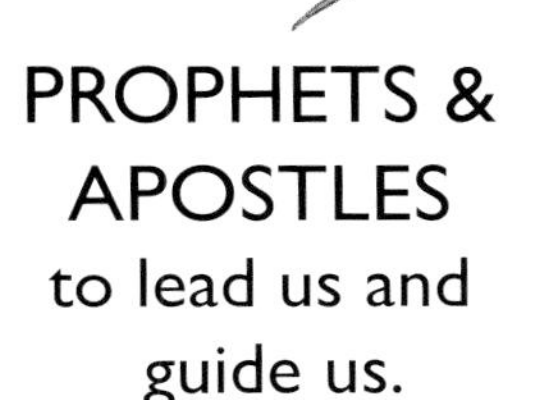

PROPHETS & APOSTLES to lead us and guide us.

SCRIPTURES to teach us and inspire us.

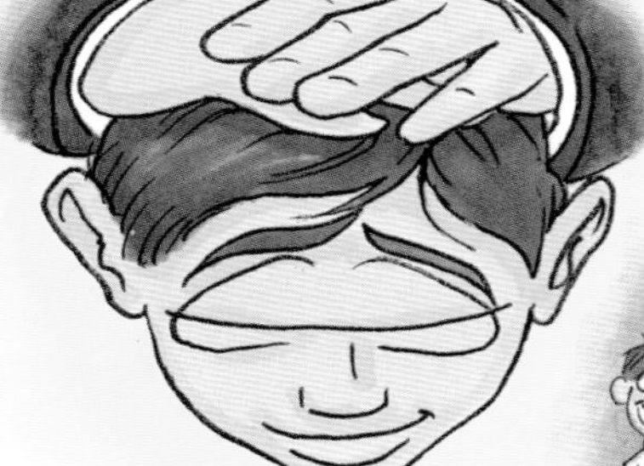

PRIESTHOOD POWER to bless us.

A WARD FAMILY to support us.

Wow! Look at all these helps you have here on earth! Heavenly Father sure does love you!

And now,
here you are,
starting your life on earth!
Even though your *spirit* has been alive for a long time, having a **body** is a brand new experience for you.
LOVIN LIFE
LOVIN LIFE
So listen to and obey your parents. They will teach you what's right and how to treat your **body**.
BODY IS A TEMPLE
Learn to love others and follow the example Jesus Christ set for you.
GIDDY-UP HORSEY!

Another one of Father's big helps is baptism and the gift of the Holy Ghost.

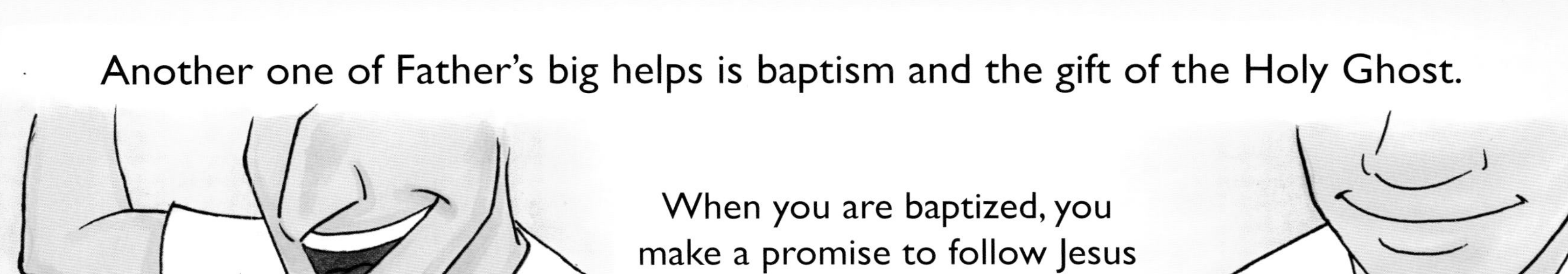


When you are baptized, you make a promise to follow Jesus for the rest of your life.

This is called your "baptismal covenant."

This covenant makes it possible to live with Heavenly Father again.

And the gift of the Holy Ghost helps you to always know and choose what's right.

Wow! With all these helps from Heavenly Father, you have a great life ahead of you

IF . . .

Heavenly Father has given all of his children AGENCY. Agency is the freedom to choose what we will do, what we will say, what we will think, and who we will become. Satan and his followers, who were cast out of heaven, tempt us to make *wrong* choices. Heavenly Father and His angels help us to make *right* choices. Learning to choose the right, even when we are tempted to make a wrong choice, is our big test on earth. What will you choose?

Will you choose to . . .
keep following the commandments as you get older?
WELCOME TO SEMINARY
SCRIPTURE MASTERY
Serve a mission?
(especially you boys)
THE PLAN OF OUR HEAVENLY FATHER
DEAR ELDER, YOU ARE CALLED TO SERVE A MISSION IN THE
MISSION
GLOP
DOINK!

Marry your sweetheart in the holy temple?
(Can you believe you will be married someday?)

REMEMBER, when you marry in the temple, you are sealed to your sweetheart. That means the two of you and your future children can all be together as a family . . . forever! This is one of the most important choices you can make in becoming like your heavenly parents!

Start a family of your own and teach your children the Great Plan of Happiness?
(Can you believe you will be a mom or dad someday?)

Follow the Lord for the rest of your life, keeping your baptismal covenant?
(Can you believe you'll be a grandma or grandpa someday?)

Of course you will choose these things! That's why you came to earth! And Heavenly Father trusts you to follow His plan.

Eventually, our **bodies** will get old and weak, and everyone who comes to earth will die. It is sad when someone we love dies.
But it helps when we remember that DEATH is part of Heavenly Father's plan and that death is NOT the end!
BODY + SPIRIT
SPIRIT
BODY
WE ♥ YOU GRAMA
Where will you go?
When you die, your *spirit* will leave your **body**. Your *spirit* will keep on living, even though your **body** is still. While your **body** stays in the ground, your *spirit* will go on to a new place.

To the SPIRIT WORLD!
The spirit world is a happy resting place for people who chose righteousness while they were on earth. You will see loved ones there who died before you did. It's a place to continue learning and growing.

Some people never had the chance to learn about Jesus Christ while they were on earth and need to be taught His gospel. So missionary work is going on in the spirit world too! If these people choose to follow Jesus in the spirit world, they can still be baptized and be sealed as families. BUT ... somebody on earth has to do it for them, inside holy temples. This is called doing work for the dead.

Everyone stays in the spirit world until that special day when each person is ...

With your *spirit* and your **body** back together again, you will be ready for . . .

# JUDGMENT

This is the day when you will look back on your life and decide if you followed Heavenly Father's Plan of Happiness. Did you make good choices on earth? Were you kind and helpful to others? Were you baptized, and did you keep your promise to try to become like Jesus? Of course you did!

And because you kept your promise at baptism, Jesus Christ will keep His promise to make you clean and pure. And now . . . you are worthy to enter . . .

# THE CELESTIAL KINGDOM!

CONGRATULATIONS!

You did it!
Your Heavenly Father
will be there to
greet you.

How do you think you
will feel when you are
back in His arms?

Just as the greatest light
comes from the sun,

the greatest happiness
and glory is in the
Celestial Kingdom.

However, not everyone will go to the Celestial Kingdom.
Some people will go to . . .

THE TERRESTRIAL KINGDOM
People who go here are good people, but they didn't accept the gospel of Jesus Christ and chose not to be baptized into His church.
Other people who go here did receive the gospel but were not valiant.
Jesus can visit those in the Terrestrial Kingdom, but Heavenly Father will not. It's a happy, beautiful place, but not nearly as glorious as the Celestial Kingdom.
MOON
GLORY-O-METER
THE TELESTIAL KINGDOM
People who go here were not faithful to Jesus. They made wrong choices and followed Satan's temptations. They can still feel the influence of the Holy Ghost, but Heavenly Father and Jesus will not go there. How sad.
STARS
GLORY-O-METER

But let's get back to the Celestial Kingdom . . . where YOU belong!
GET DOWN SAMUEL
DEJA VU
LOOK!
YOU WERE SO SCARED!
AND NOBODY WAS KILLED ???

Here you will enjoy Eternal Life, the greatest of all God's gifts! That means . . .
You will live forever with your Heavenly Father and Jesus Christ.
You will live forever with family members who were sealed to you in the holy temple.
You will become heavenly parents and have spirit children, just as your heavenly parents did back in the premortal world.
And you will have a fulness of joy
All because you followed the Great Plan of Happiness.

Wow! What an exciting journey you are on! Now you know . . .

Where you came from,

why you are here on earth,

and what is possible in the next life.

Heavenly Father loves you and trusts you to follow His Great Plan of Happiness.

And, just as its name says, it will bring YOU the most happiness now and forever!

Learn it. Love it. Live it.

# FHE Lesson Helps—The Great Plan of Happiness

## SONGS:

| | |
|---|---|
| "I Am a Child of God" | Hymn 301 |
| "I Know My Father Lives" | Hymn 302 |
| "Families Can Be Together Forever" | Hymn 300 |
| "O My Father" | Hymn 292 |
| "I Lived in Heaven" | *Children's Songbook,* 4 |
| "The Family Is of God" | *Friend*, Oct. 2008, 28–29 |

## THIS IS YOUR LIFE: A GRAND THREE-ACT PLAY

Elder Boyd K. Packer gives a great analogy of how our life is really a three-act play ("The Play and the Plan," Church Educational System Fireside for College-Age Young Adults, 7 May 1995, 2). Knowing what happens in all three acts helps us make sense of our life here on earth (Act 2). Act out the three-act play with your family. Assign characters, have a narrator, make it a melodrama (with cheering and booing), and have fun with it! Below is an outline, with scripture references and quotes (to act as segues leading to the next act) to use as you see fit.

*"Man, as a spirit, was . . . born of Heavenly Parents, and reared to maturity in the eternal mansions of the Father."*

—First Presidency (*Origin of Man,* 1909)

### ACT 1—PRE-MORTAL LIFE

*Abraham 3:22–26* (Noble and great spirits; Earth created as testing ground for us.)

*Moses 4:1–4* (Council in Heaven, Satan rebels and is cast out.)

*Bible Dictionary, "War in Heaven"* (GREAT overall resource!)

*"When we pass from pre-existence to mortality, we bring with us the traits and talents there developed."*

—Elder Bruce R. McConkie (*Mortal Messiah,* 1:23)

### ACT 2—EARTH LIFE

*Alma 7:11–13* (Christ suffered for us; the Atonement.)

*2 Nephi 2:25–27* (Happiness is our purpose; Jesus Christ redeems us; we have agency.)

*2 Nephi 31:17, 21* (We should follow Christ's example: repent, be baptized, and endure to the end.)

*"Nothing is going to startle us more when we pass through the veil to the other side than to realize how well we know our Father and how familiar His face is to us."*

—President Ezra Taft Benson (*Ensign,* July 1975, 62)

### ACT 3 —POSTMORTAL WORLD

#### SPIRIT WORLD

*Alma 40:11–12* (When we die, we go to the spirit world.)

#### RESURRECTION/JUDGMENT

*Alma 11:42–44* (Everyone will be resurrected and will be judged.)

#### CELESTIAL KINGDOM

*D&C 76:58, 62, 69–70* (Blessings of the celestial kingdom)

*D&C 131:1–2* (Temple marriage required for exaltation)

*D&C 14:7* (Eternal Life is the greatest gift of all)

*"As man now is, God once was; As God now is, man may become."*

—President Lorenzo Snow

# GAINING PERSPECTIVE

Two lesson ideas to help your family gain a sense of eternity and the IMPORTANCE of their earth life NOW!

## STRINGING IT OUT

Have two family members **stretch a piece of string or yarn the entire length of the room,** each holding one end of the string. Have everyone imagine that at one end of the string, the string doesn't stop. Instead, it keeps going through the wall, into the next room, and out of the house. Imagine that the string continues stretching across your town, across your state, and out into space (it doesn't follow the contour of the earth). It keeps going past the moon, the planets, the solar system, the galaxy, and so on. It goes on FOREVER. Wow!

Have everyone imagine that the other end of the string does the same thing—it goes on FOREVER as well.

Then, string a ring (wedding or CTR ring), centering it in the middle of the string. Explain that the entire string represents a time-line of your life (which is eternity) and that the width of the ring represents the time you spend on earth. One side of the string is your premortal life and everything you did there was preparing you for your time here on earth. The other side is your postmortal life, and what happens there pretty much depends on what you do with your earth life. Everything points to this incredibly short time spent on earth. Discuss how IMPORTANT your time is right now on earth and how to make the most of it (make right choices, build faith, repent, and so forth)!

## WAIT & SKATE

Have each family member **imagine he or she is a world class figure skater.** (Draw out the story, get your kids into it, and make it fun!) You have trained your entire life for a mere three minutes out on the ice to prove your stuff and bring home that gold medal. The night of the Olympic competition finally arrives and you begin your routine (have kids act out their figure skating "tricks" in the middle of the room, like spins and triple klutzes. Oh, I mean lutzes). Everything is going perfectly, until suddenly, you catch a smell of someone eating a big, juicy hamburger right on the front row (Dad acts this out). It smells so good! You are so hungry! Ask the kids, *"Would you stop right in the middle of your routine, skate over to this person (Dad), and ask him to share his burger with you?"* Discuss how ridiculous this would be with the music still playing and millions of people watching while you munch on this hamburger.

**Make the analogy:** How equally ridiculous is the idea that anyone who has been preparing ALL his premortal life for this short routine called earth life, to prove himself and return with honor to Heavenly Father, would ever give that up for a momentary "appetite" (temptation) he feels he's just "gotta have" right now. There is too much at stake!

One last great quote from President Monson:

*"We are sons and daughters of a living God in whose image we are created. Think of that truth: 'Created in the image of God!' We cannot sincerely hold this conviction without experiencing a profound new sense of strength and power, even the strength to live the commandments of God, the power to resist the temptations of Satan."*

—President Thomas S. Monson (*Pathways to Perfection*)

## Find the SMILEYS 

Happiness is found all throughout our Heavenly Father's plan. See if you can find a smiley face on each page. And because the Celestial Kingdom is the happiest of all, there are 10 smileys for you to find on that page (p. 28). Happy searching!